THIRTY MINUTES TOO LATE

MINDWORK PUBLISHING

MINDWORK PUBLISHING LLC

Published by Mindwork Publishing

ISBN: 979-8-9992682-3-5

Scripture theme inspired by Proverbs 6:6–8.

Printed in the United States of America

First edition

CONTENTS

Proverbs 6:6–8

Look at the ant and learn.

The ant does not wait for someone to force it to work.

It does not need a boss watching every move.

It prepares ahead of time. It handles what needs to be handled before it is too late.

This book is inspired by the wisdom of Proverbs 6:6–8.

CHAPTER ONE

SNOOZE BUTTON LIFE

The alarm screamed. Sakari smacked her phone until it stopped and squinted at the time. 11:00 AM. Sunlight cut across her floor, lighting up the mess, tangled clothes, scattered notebooks, a laundry basket tipped sideways against her desk .Her eyes landed on the space heater. Too close to her socks. Again. She stepped over the extension cord her dad kept warning her about and made a mental note to deal with all of it later. Later felt very far away. The couch downstairs felt very close. She went to the couch. She stayed there for a long time. Eventually, her stomach complained loudly enough to win.

In the kitchen, she cracked two eggs into a pan and laid a tortilla flat across the top. The sizzle filled the room. Her mind drifted to last weekend, when she'd walked away from the stove with the burner still going. Her mom had found it.

"Sakari. You cannot just walk away from heat. One day, you will start a fire."

Sakari had rolled her eyes. She rolled them again now, just remembering it.

She carried her burrito back to the couch, pulled a blanket over her shoulders, and turned on the TV. Reruns played. A laugh track went off every thirty seconds. She picked up her phone and scrolled.

Homework sat in her backpack. Her room sat messy upstairs. She scrolled anyway.

A ping broke through the noise.

Angie: *Hey, you alive? Wanna hang today?*

Sakari smiled. She pictured the two of them at the mall, bubble tea, walking slow, making fun of everything in the sale bins. She typed back:

Sorry, swamped with chores

A thumbs-up appeared. No words.

Guilt settled in her stomach like a stone.

Another ping. Mom this time.

Mom: *You didn't clean your room yet, did you? Responsibility before relaxation, remember.*

Sakari dropped her phone face-down on the cushion.

The front door swung open. Her dad walked in, gym bag over one shoulder, hair still damp.

"Hey, sleepyhead." He kicked off his shoes. "Productive morning?"

Sakari sat up halfway. "Yeah. Honoring the Sabbath. Rest day."

He raised an eyebrow but smiled anyway. "Cool. Just make sure the homework gets done before Monday."

They both laughed. It was a good moment, until it wasn't.

"Hey, Kari?" He set his bag down. "Got a fraud alert on the card. Declined me at the gas station."

Her stomach dropped straight through the couch cushions.

"Oh," she said. "I ordered pizza last night."

He breathed out slowly through his nose. "Next time, ask. That's all I'm saying."

He headed upstairs. The room felt quieter after he left.

Sakari opened her phone. A reminder sat at the top of her screen.

History Project Due Monday.

She dismissed it.

FlixFlow took over from there. One episode turned into three. Plot twists stacked on top of each other. She ate chips she didn't remember grabbing. The afternoon light shifted from gold to gray outside the window.

"Your mom will be home in thirty minutes." Her dad's voice came from the top of the stairs. "Go clean that war zone."

Thirty minutes.

The words landed hard.

Sakari shot up, grabbed the remote, and sprinted upstairs. Her room looked exactly the way she'd left it, like a storm had moved through and decided to stay. She worked fast. Clothes into the hamper. Books stacked. Pens shoved into her pencil cup. She moved in quick bursts, her heart hammering the whole time.

She threw herself onto her bed and caught her breath.

Then the door opened.

Her mom's face said it all before she said a word.

"How many times, Sakari." Her voice came out low and tired. "How many times have I asked you to clean before I get home?"

"Mom, I did clean, "

"And three burned-out candle stubs on your windowsill? Are you trying to burn this house down?"

"I was just taking a break. I handled it."

"A break." Her mom repeated the words slowly. "You had the entire day."

"I was *going* to, "

"That's all I hear from you. 'I was going to.' Every single time."

Something cracked open in Sakari's chest. "I'm drowning, okay?!" The words came out louder than she planned. "School, college apps, chores, everyone wants something from me. I do one thing and it's still never enough!"

Her mom's eyes filled. The anger shifted into something sadder and harder to look at.

"Then tell me what it is," her mom said quietly. "Because I don't recognize you right now. You used to care, about yourself, about this family. Now every day feels like waiting for the next thing to go wrong."

The silence that followed sat heavier than any argument.

"It's not like that, Mom," Sakari whispered.

"Did you finish your history project?"

Her shoulders fell.

"No."

Her mom walked out without another word.

Sakari sat still for a minute. Then she got up and cleaned, all the way this time. She moved the space heater to the far wall. She coiled the extension cord and tucked it out of the walkway. She found an old candle under her bed, *Avril Lavender*, the label half-peeled off.

Her mom's voice came back to her: *Never leave candles unattended.*

She lit it anyway and set it on the windowsill. The smell spread through the room, soft and warm. She stepped back and looked around.

Clean. Actually clean.

"Mom!" she called.

Her mom appeared in the doorway with her arms crossed, braced. Then she stopped.

"Oh wow." She looked around the room. "Look at this."

Sakari smiled. "Dad had a point."

Her mom laughed a little. "And it smells good, too." She pointed at the candle. "Blow that out before you leave though, okay?"

"I will."

Later, her dad knocked. "We're heading out. Food's downstairs if you want to make dinner."

"Sure."

The door clicked shut. Sakari looked at the kitchen and thought about cooking. Then she opened the food app, tapped through to her favorite pizza place, and put in her order. The doorbell rang twenty minutes later.

She ate on the couch. The show picked up where she'd left it.

Her phone buzzed.

Mom: *Did you blow out that candle?*

Sakari's thumb hovered.

In a few minutes.

Mom: *Now, please.*

Okay, okay.

She didn't move. The episode was getting good. The next one started automatically.

Ten minutes passed.

Mom: *Sakari. Did you blow out the candle. Yes or no.*

On my way upstairs now.

She wasn't.

She fell asleep on the couch with her phone in her hand and FlixFlow still playing.

The front door opened.

"Sakari."

Her mom's voice cut straight through sleep. Sakari blinked and sat up.

Her parents stood in the doorway. Her dad's jaw was tight. Her mom's eyes moved from Sakari, to the pizza boxes, to the unread messages on the phone screen, to the ceiling, toward the upstairs room, where a candle still burned on the windowsill.

All the things Sakari had said she would do sat in a pile around her.

CHAPTER TWO

CRACKS IN THE MIRROR

"**S**akari!"

Her dad's voice filled the house. Sakari jolted upright on the couch, heart already pounding before she was fully awake.

He stepped inside and let the door swing shut behind him. His eyes moved from her, to the pizza boxes on the coffee table, to the ceiling, toward the candle still burning upstairs.

"We walk in and you're knocked out on the couch. Lit candle upstairs." He kept his voice low and tight, like he was working hard to hold it there. "And you used my card again without asking. That's why it got declined at dinner tonight."

Sakari sat up straight. "I'm sorry. I didn't mean to, I'll pay you back."

"Sakari." He shook his head. "I'm not talking about the money. I'm talking about trust. Blow out the candle. Ask before you spend. Two things. You couldn't do either one."

Her mom stepped in behind him, arms folded, face calm in that way that meant she was done arguing. "Clean this up," she said. "Then go to your room. We'll talk tomorrow."

Sakari nodded. She gathered the pizza boxes and wiped crumbs from the table. Every movement felt slow and waterlogged, like her body was carrying extra weight. She went upstairs, blew out the candle, and watched the little flame disappear.

The lavender smell made her stomach turn.

She got into bed and stared at the ceiling. The house was completely quiet. The quiet pressed down harder than any yelling would have.

Morning came slow and gray. No parents moving around downstairs, no smell of breakfast. Just Sakari and the stale feeling of having messed up.

She thought about going down to apologize. The thought sat in her chest, uncomfortable. *Later. There's still time.*

The doorbell rang.

She shuffled to the door in her robe. Angie stood on the porch, notebook tucked under her arm, a bright look on her face that didn't match how Sakari felt at all.

"Hey! Hope I'm not too early." Angie held up the notebook. "Figured we could knock out the second half of the history project."

Sakari blinked. "Right. The project."

Angie's smile dropped. "Please tell me you did your part."

Sakari looked off to the side.

Angie stepped inside and set her stuff down on the table with a thud. "Seriously? We planned this a week ago. My grade is attached to yours."

"I know. I'll get it done. Just, "

"Don't say chill." Angie pointed at her. "You keep putting things off. At some point, it lands on me too."

Sakari opened her laptop. "Fine. Let's just work."

They sat side by side for almost an hour, mostly quiet. Keyboards clicking, pages turning. Slowly, the project took shape.

Then Sakari looked up. "Did you know Abraham, from the Bible, was from Mesopotamia?"

Angie squinted. "Wait. Mesopotamia shows up in the Bible?"

"Yeah. He was from this city called Ur. The whole ancient world kind of connects."

Angie leaned over to look at her screen. "That's actually really interesting."

Something loosened between them. They kept working, and for a while, the room felt easier.

The front door opened that afternoon. Her parents walked in, and Angie jumped up immediately.

"Hi, Mr. and Mrs. Johnson! Just helping Sakari get the project finished."

Her dad smiled, small, but real. "Good. Glad someone's keeping her on track."

Angie laughed a little awkwardly. "She's doing okay today."

Sakari smiled and said nothing.

When Angie packed up to leave, she paused at the door. "Project's due tomorrow. Don't forget your half." She pointed. "I love you. Do not blow this."

"I won't," Sakari said.

Her dad was in the hallway when she turned around.

"Hey, Dad. How was church?"

He looked at her for a moment before answering. "Sakari. We need to talk."

The floor shifted under her feet.

"Why did you order food when the fridge was full? Why did you use my card without asking? Why was that candle still burning when we got home?"

"I didn't feel like cooking. And I was going to blow it out, I just fell asleep."

"You always fall asleep. You always didn't feel like it." He crossed his arms. "I'm tired of the same explanation, Sakari."

"I said I'd pay you back."

"With what? Your allowance?"

Her jaw tightened. "Maybe if you gave me more freedom, "

"Freedom." He said the word flat. "You used my card without permission. You left a fire burning in your room. That's not a freedom issue. That's a responsibility issue."

Her mom's voice came from upstairs. "Enough. I can hear both of you from here."

Sakari pointed at her dad. "He started it."

"Oh, come on!" He threw his hands up. "I'm the bad guy now?"

Her mom appeared at the top of the stairs. "Sakari. He has a point. You know he has a point."

"I'm trying! Nobody sees that. Everyone just lines up to tell me what I did wrong."

She turned and went to her room and slammed the door behind her.

"HEY." Her dad's voice hit the door like a fist. "We do not slam doors in this house!"

Sakari stood in the middle of her room, chest heaving. Same argument. Same ending. Her messing up, them getting frustrated, her feeling cornered.

She flopped onto her bed.

Angie's voice came back to her: *Don't blow this.*

Her phone buzzed. A school alert, Part 1 of the History Project due by 4 PM tomorrow. No late submissions.

The books and papers on her desk sat exactly where she'd left them.

She picked up the remote.

One episode. Then I'll start.

One turned into two. Two turned into six. At 7 PM her mom called from the kitchen.

"Dinner's ready!"

"Not hungry!"

Her mom sighed loud enough to hear through the wall. "Don't stay up all night."

Sakari turned off the TV at 2 AM, eyes burning, the project still not done.

10:12 AM.

She sat straight up in bed like someone had grabbed her by the collar. First period was already halfway over.

She sprinted downstairs. Her dad was at his desk, papers spread in front of him.

"Dad. I need a ride to school."

He looked up slowly. "You overslept."

"I know. Please, can we just go?"

He checked his watch and rubbed his forehead. "I have a client in thirty minutes. You're pushing my whole morning back."

"I'm sorry. Can we please just go?"

The drive was silent. No music. No talking. Just traffic lights and the sound of the engine.

She slipped into third-period English. Mrs. Handmaker didn't look up from the board.

"Glad you could join us."

Sakari dropped into the seat next to Angie.

"What happened?" Angie whispered.

"I fell asleep too late. Overslept."

Angie made a face. "Again?"

"Do we still have until the end of the day for the project?"

"Mr. Hatala said this was the final extension. No more."

Sakari reached into her backpack. Dug around. Dug around again.

Her stomach fell straight to the floor.

The project was still at home. Sitting on her desk, right where she'd left it.

"I forgot it," she said quietly.

Angie stared at her. "You're joking."

"I didn't mean to. I just, "

"You *just*." Angie's voice sharpened. "You always *just*." She pulled her bag into her lap. "I told Mr. Hatala you were reliable. I defended you."

"I'll fix it. I'll figure it out."

"Figure it out, then."

Mrs. Handmaker glanced over. "Girls. Take it to the hall."

They stepped outside. The door clicked shut behind them.

Angie turned to face her. "You say you're overwhelmed. Okay. But so is everyone. Everyone is tired. Everyone has stuff. You keep dropping things that land on other people."

"I'll get it to him. I promise."

"You'd better." Angie shook her head. "I can't keep holding your end too."

She walked back inside.

Sakari stood alone in the hallway. She reached for her phone to call her dad.

Dead. No charge.

She looked down at her empty backpack.

Down the empty hallway.

The bell schedule on the wall.

Everything she'd said she would do sat behind her like a trail of dropped things. And somewhere up ahead, a deadline was running out.

Chapter Three

Up in Smoke

Sakari slid down against the lockers and let the cold metal hold her up.

Angie's words sat in her chest like a splinter. *I can't keep holding your end too.*

The bell rang. Last period. P.E.

She grabbed her bag and walked to the gym.

Mr. Trent spotted her the second she came through the doors.

"Sakari! Tell me you're not ducking track tryouts again."

She gave him half a smile. "Coach. You know that's not my thing."

"Funny." He pointed to the cones set up across the court. "Because you've got the fastest footwork in this building. Get out there. Run something off."

She obeyed without arguing.

The drills moved her body on autopilot, jogging the baseline, shuffling through the cone pattern, cutting left, cutting right. Her feet knew what to do. Her mind went somewhere else entirely.

I'll fix it.

I always say that.

What if this time I actually can't?

She ran anyway.

After class, she hung back by the lockers longer than she needed to. Angie left with a group of girls without looking her way. Sakari pretended not to notice.

The bus ride home felt long. She kept her head against the window and watched the neighborhood scroll past, driveways, mailboxes, kids on bikes. Her legs bounced the whole way, a restless energy with nowhere to go.

She stepped off at her stop, exhaled, and walked up the driveway.

The house was quiet. She dropped her backpack by the front door and went upstairs.

Her room looked exactly the way she'd left it. Clean. Organized. Every surface wiped down and every item in its place.

It felt wrong somehow. Like a stage set for a play she wasn't in.

She crossed to the window and pushed it open. Cool air moved through the curtains and touched her face. She stood there for a moment and breathed.

Then her eyes landed on the matchbox.

The Avril Lavender candle sat on the windowsill right where she'd left it.

Don't. Just breathe.

She looked around. The room smelled stale, old takeout and trapped air.

She struck a match.

She set the candle near the windowsill, stepped back, and told herself: *Just a few minutes. Just until it smells okay in here.*

Downstairs, she built a sandwich she didn't really want and wrapped herself in the couch blanket. FlixFlow started up. Characters argued and kissed and got into car chases. She watched without watching.

Her eyes drifted to the stairs.

Go blow it out.

She pulled the blanket tighter.

In a minute.

Her dad's voice surfaced from somewhere: *We can't afford to be careless, Kari. You know that.*

She stood halfway.

Sat back down.

It's fine. I'll handle it.

The next episode started on its own. The room got dim as the sun shifted. Her breathing slowed.

Her eyes closed.

She woke up choking.

The smell hit her before anything else, thick and sour, coating the back of her throat. Then the heat. Then the orange glow dancing across the living room walls.

She jolted upright.

"Mom?! Dad?!"

Silence.

Smoke pressed down from the ceiling. The living room flickered with reflected light. Her heart hammered so hard she felt it in her ears.

She ran for the stairs.

The hallway upstairs glowed. Flames crawled along the bottom edge of her bedroom door, licking the frame, reaching for the carpet.

She stopped. Backed away. Coughing.

She turned and ran for the front door instead, fumbling with the knob, throwing it open, and stumbled out onto the front lawn, dropping to her knees in the grass.

Behind her, the fire found the upstairs windows.

She turned around and stared.

Her room. Her journals. The photos from when she was little, the ones in the box on her closet shelf. All of it glowing orange and black.

She ran next door and beat her fist against Mrs. Maxwell's door until it swung open.

"Sakari, what on earth, "

"I left a candle. My room. It's on fire."

Mrs. Maxwell grabbed her arm and pulled her inside. "Call 911. Use my phone. Right now."

Sakari's hands shook so badly she nearly dropped it. The dispatcher's voice came through steady and calm. Sakari's voice came through broken and small. She gave the address. She answered the questions.

Then she called her dad.

Ten minutes later, tires screamed against the pavement out front.

Her dad was out of the car before it fully stopped. "Sakari!"

She ran straight into him and broke apart completely, sobbing into his shoulder, barely able to form words.

"I didn't mean to, I just lit it for a minute, just for the smell, I was going to blow it out, I swear, "

He pulled back and looked at the house. His face went completely still.

Fire trucks lined the street. Hoses stretched across the lawn. Smoke poured from the upstairs windows in dark rolling columns. The second floor was fully burning.

Her mom's car came around the corner fast. She parked crooked and ran toward them.

"What happened?"

Her dad didn't answer right away. "It's gone," he finally said.

Sakari's voice came out as a whisper. "I lit the candle. And I fell asleep."

Her mom pressed both hands over her mouth. Her eyes filled.

A fire captain walked over, helmet in hand. "We've got it contained. But the structure's compromised. Most of the upper floor is lost."

Nobody said anything.

Firefighters moved past them with equipment. Radios crackled. Water rushed through hoses. Lights strobed red and white across the neighbors' faces, everyone standing on their lawns watching.

Sakari looked at her parents.

Her dad stood still with his arms at his sides, staring at the house.

Her mom had turned away.

And Sakari stood between them, covered in the smell of smoke, with nothing left to say that would matter.

The hotel room smelled like cleaning products and recycled air. Two double beds. A TV bolted to the wall. A window with a parking lot view.

Her dad stood at the window with his back to the room.

Sakari sat on the edge of the bed. "I know sorry doesn't fix it. But I, "

"I don't want to hear sorry right now."

His voice wasn't loud. That made it harder.

Her mom sat on the other bed with her hands folded in her lap, looking at the floor. "We'll figure out the logistics tomorrow. Get some sleep."

Sakari pulled back the stiff hotel sheets and lay down without changing. The smell of smoke still lived in her hair, in her clothes, in her skin.

She stared at the ceiling.

The room was completely quiet.

And the quiet told her everything she'd spent the whole day trying not to hear.

Chapter Four

Ashes and Revelations

The hotel ceiling was beige. Plain and flat and completely uninteresting. Sakari stared at it anyway.

The sheets smelled like bleach. The air conditioner rattled in the corner, pushing the same cold air around in circles. Her parents sat on the other bed, scrolling through their phones in silence.

No one spoke. No one looked her way.

She pulled the comforter over her face and lay very still and pretended to be asleep.

By noon they were standing in front of the house.

What was left of it.

Charred beams crossed the sky where the roof used to be. The windows were just dark, jagged frames.

Smoke stains spread up the outer walls like black bruises. The front door hung open, and through it, everything was gray and wet and ruined.

Her mom stepped inside first. Her sneakers crunched through soaked ash.

Her dad followed. His shoulders were tight, his jaw set.

Sakari came in last, arms wrapped around herself.

The couch was a tangle of springs and soot. The refrigerator door hung loose from one hinge. The smell of smoke had soaked into every surface, into the walls, into the air itself.

Her mom stopped in the kitchen and bent down. When she stood back up, she held a scorched spoon, turning it over in her fingers without expression.

Sakari moved down the hall toward her room.

She almost didn't recognize it.

Her foot kicked something soft on the floor. She looked down.

Mr. Buttons. Her first teddy bear, the one from the photo on her old dresser. One ear melted. One eye gone. The stuffing pushed out through a split in the seam.

She picked him up.

Her dad's voice broke through the silence behind her, low and raw. "Years of work. All of it gone."

A crash. He'd kicked a pile of debris. His foot hit a beam and sent ash rising in a cloud.

Sakari didn't move.

He stood still for a moment. Then crouched and reached into the ash and pulled something out. A photograph, burned dark around all four edges. He looked at it for a long time before folding it carefully and slipping it into his pocket.

"I told you to blow out that candle." He didn't look at her. "You said you would."

"I know," she said.

Her mom appeared in the doorway. "We lost everything in this house."

"I know."

"Do you?"

Sakari looked up. Her mom's eyes were wet, but her face was still. Hard and careful, the way a person looks when they are holding themselves together by force.

"I didn't mean for this to happen," Sakari said. "I just forgot."

Her mom's voice came back quiet and clear. "That's not good enough."

Nobody argued with that. There was nothing to argue.

They met with the insurance adjuster in the hotel lobby that afternoon. He had a neat tie and a folder full of papers and a polite smile that stopped right below his eyes.

"Unfortunately," he said, "your policy lapsed last month. The grace period had already expired before the incident."

Her dad's jaw tightened. "So we're not covered."

"I'm afraid not."

Her mom stood slowly. "We get nothing?"

"You're welcome to file an appeal. But I can't promise coverage." He closed the folder. "I'm sorry."

Her parents sat without moving after he left. The lobby noise continued around them, elevator dings, rolling luggage, a kid laughing somewhere near the vending machines.

Sakari sat across from them and looked at her hands.

The weight of it pressed down and kept pressing.

That night the hotel room felt smaller than before.

Sakari curled into the far corner of her bed, knees pulled to her chest, Mr. Buttons tucked under her arm. Her mom sat by the window with a book open in her lap. Her dad lay on top of the covers on the other bed, staring straight up.

"I'm sorry," Sakari said.

The air conditioner hummed.

"I'm really sorry. I know that doesn't fix anything. I know you might not be ready to hear it." She kept going anyway. "But I want you to know, I want to fix it. Whatever I can."

Nothing.

"I've been messing up for a long time. Not just yesterday. I've been selfish. I kept putting things off and telling myself it was fine and it wasn't fine." Her voice stayed steady. "I didn't care enough until everything was already gone."

Her dad didn't respond. He didn't turn away either.

She hugged the burned teddy bear and listened to the room breathe.

Sleep stayed far away.

The TV murmured through the wall from the next room. The air conditioner rattled on. An ant moved across the nightstand in a straight, deliberate line. Sakari watched it for a moment, then slid open the nightstand drawer to look for something, anything, to do.

A Bible. Cover worn soft from years of hands.

She almost closed the drawer.

She picked it up instead.

The pages fanned open somewhere in the middle and her eyes landed on a bold header: *Proverbs 6.*

She skimmed down the page and one line stopped her completely.

Go to the ant, you lazy bum. Watch its ways, and become wise.

She shut the book.

Opened it again.

Read the line three more times.

The ant doesn't wait to be told. The ant doesn't say *in a minute* or *I was going to* or *I'll handle it later.* The ant just moves. Every day. Without being asked.

She pulled out her phone and opened a new note.

Things I Will Not Let Burn Again

☐ Trust

☐ Friendship

☐ My future

☐ My family

She stared at the list. Then added one more line at the bottom.

☐ Start becoming wise.

She sat with it for a while.

Then she opened her messages and found Angie's name.

Hey. I owe you more than an apology. Can we talk tomorrow? I understand if you're done with me. But I'm ready to actually change.

She set the phone face-up on the nightstand and watched the screen go dark.

No reply came. That was okay.

She'd said the true thing. She'd written the list. She'd taken the first step without knowing what came next, which was, she realized, exactly what the ant would do.

She pulled the covers up and closed her eyes.

Chapter Five

SMOKE TRAILS AND CHECKLISTS

The morning air hit her face the second she stepped outside. Her hoodie wasn't quite enough for it. She pulled the sleeves down over her hands and started walking.

Ten minutes to the library. It felt longer.

Her sneakers scraped the sidewalk. A dog threw itself against a fence as she passed. Someone across the street laughed at something, loud and sudden, and her shoulders jumped.

What if Angie doesn't want to see me?

Her phone buzzed.

Angie: *I'm still at the library if you want to talk.*

Sakari stopped walking, read the message twice, and typed back:

On my way.

She walked faster.

The library doors slid open with a soft whoosh. Cool air and the smell of old paper and printer ink. Quiet in the way that only libraries are quiet, full of small sounds that somehow add up to nothing.

Angie sat at a corner table, earbuds out, watching her walk over.

"Hey," Sakari said.

"Hey."

She sat down. Her fingers found each other in her lap and twisted. "I didn't come here with excuses."

"Good," Angie said.

"I just needed to say, you were right. About all of it. I've been dropping the ball and expecting you to pick it up."

Angie crossed her arms. "I'm listening."

"I always played it off like I didn't care. But the truth is I got scared." Sakari looked at the table. "Scared of actually trying and still failing. So I stopped trying at all. That wasn't fair to you."

Angie's expression stayed steady, but something in it shifted, barely, like a door opening one inch. "You didn't just make me frustrated. You disappeared. And when you did show up, everything was already on fire."

Sakari nodded slowly. "I know."

She breathed in. "Our house actually caught fire two nights ago. Because I left a candle burning and fell asleep." She kept her eyes on the table. "We lost almost everything inside."

Silence.

"I've never felt regret like that before. It changed something." She looked up. "I don't want to keep being that person."

Angie stared at her. "Wait, your actual house?"

"Yeah."

"Sakari." Angie sat back. "Are you okay?"

"I don't know yet. But I'm trying to figure it out."

A long pause stretched between them. Angie looked out the window, then back.

"I'm really sorry that happened," she said, quieter now. "I wish you'd told me sooner."

Sakari pulled out her phone and slid it across the table. "I made a list."

Angie looked down at the screen. *Things I Will Not Let Burn Again.*

"That's a lot," Angie said.

"I know it sounds corny."

"A little." Angie almost smiled. She read through it. Trust. Friendship. My future. My family. Start becoming wise.

She set the phone down. "I'm still upset about the project. And about how things have been." She folded her hands on the table. "But I'm not going to pretend I don't care what happened to you."

"I know."

"If you're actually serious about changing, I'll be here for that. But I won't drag you." Angie held her gaze. "We clear?"

"We're clear."

Angie gave one firm nod. "Then let's fix the project. I can tell Mr. Hatala you had a family emergency, but the whole thing has to be done by Monday. No more extensions. We're both on the line."

"I'll pull my weight this time," Sakari said. "You have my word."

Angie studied her face for a moment, searching for the truth in it. Whatever she found there was enough.

"Okay," she said. "Then let's get to work."

Back at the hotel, Sakari dropped her bag onto the bed.

It still smelled like smoke.

She unzipped it and turned it over. Crumpled papers, broken pencil stubs, a granola bar that had been completely crushed into a corner. She pulled everything out one piece at a time, sorted it, threw away what was trash, and set aside what still mattered.

Then she grabbed a pen and the hotel notepad from the nightstand.

Checklist – Today

☐ Contact Mr. Hatala

☐ Text Nana

☐ Find clean clothes

☐ Re-outline project slides

☐ Research college requirements

She looked at the list. Five things. Real things she could actually do today.

She picked up her phone and started at the top.

That evening her dad walked into the room and stopped.

Papers stacked on the table. A flash drive labeled in her handwriting. Her laptop open to a slide deck.

"You working on something?"

"School project." She didn't look up. "Trying to catch up."

He stood there for a moment. "Good."

He didn't say *I forgive you*. He didn't say everything was okay.

But he sat down in the chair by the window instead of leaving the room. And that was something.

Later, after he'd fallen asleep and the room was dark and quiet, Sakari picked up the notepad. She added one more line at the bottom of the list.

☐ Earn back Dad's trust.

Then she went back up to the top and started checking things off.

✔ Contact Mr. Hatala

✔ Text Nana

✔ Find clean clothes

✔ Re-outline project slides

✔ Research college requirements

Five small checkmarks. Five things she'd said she would do and actually did.

She looked at the one empty box at the bottom.

Tomorrow, she thought. *That one starts tomorrow.*

She set the notepad on the nightstand, turned off the lamp, and closed her eyes.

For the first time in a long time, tomorrow felt like something worth getting up for.

CHAPTER SIX

EMBERS AND ECHOES

The mirror showed her someone who looked almost normal.

Sakari tugged her hoodie sleeves down over her wrists and studied her reflection. The hoodie smelled like detergent, clean and plain and good. Her mom had taken her to a discount store that morning for a few basics. Enough to get by.

She looked half-confident. Half-exhausted. Both felt honest.

"You ready?" Her dad stood in the doorway.

"Yeah."

The community center sat across town, a pop-up relief hub run by volunteers, set up in a building that usually hosted basketball leagues and after-school programs. Her parents needed help sorting through aid options. Sakari had asked to come.

She wanted to be useful. She also just wanted to be there, in the room, present, which she was starting to understand was its own kind of thing.

Inside, the place moved.

Voices layered over each other in a low hum. Clipboards clattered. Sneakers squeaked across tile floors. The smell of old coffee and fresh paint mixed together in a way that shouldn't have worked but did. Folding tables held stacks of flyers. Along the walls, boxes of canned food and donated clothes were sorted into rows.

Her mom checked in at the front table. Her dad found a woman in a yellow vest and spread a housing list between them.

Sakari drifted toward the far corner, where someone had set up a small reading nook for kids. A few picture books had toppled sideways. She crouched and started straightening them, sorting by size, grouping by color.

A woman nearby looked up from a box of puzzle pieces. "You here to help?"

Sakari glanced up. "Yeah. Just trying to pitch in."

The woman pointed. "Grab those empty bins then. More books coming in from the donation drop."

Sakari grabbed the bins.

The work was simple. Stack, sort, label, move. Nothing dramatic about it. But something about the rhythm felt good, her hands doing something useful, her feet planted somewhere real.

She stayed at it for over an hour.

That afternoon, her mom found her and pressed a small plastic folder into her hands.

"Hotel extension papers. We got approved for another week."

Sakari took it and held it carefully. "That's good."

Her mom looked at her, really looked, the way she used to when Sakari was little and had done something worth noticing.

"I'm proud of how you've been showing up," she said.

Sakari blinked. "Really?"

"I mean it. You're making effort. That counts."

Something opened up in her chest. Warm and unfamiliar. She didn't have the right words for it, so she just nodded and held onto the folder a little tighter.

Back at the hotel, she sat cross-legged at the foot of the bed with her laptop. Angie had already emailed the updated slides.

Sakari read through them, added her section of notes, smoothed out a few transitions, and sent it back.

A reply came ten minutes later.

Angie: *Looks good. Thanks for actually doing your part this time :)*

Sakari smiled at the screen.

She clicked over to her grades page. Most of them were still rough. She didn't look away or close the tab. She just looked at the numbers and let them be true.

Two assignments now showed *Complete.*

Two. A start.

Her dad came in that evening carrying a takeout bag. He set it on the table without ceremony.

"Got your favorite. Grilled cheese and tomato soup."

Sakari looked at the bag. "Seriously?"

"Thought you'd earned it."

She grinned. "Thanks, Dad."

They ate side by side on the edge of the bed, bowls balanced on their knees. The room was quiet. Not the heavy, loaded quiet from before, just the regular kind, two people eating dinner, nothing needing to be said.

It felt like breathing normally after holding your breath for a long time.

Before she turned out the light, she pulled out the hotel notepad and wrote a fresh checklist.

Tomorrow

☐ Finish project slides

☐ Help at the center

☐ Email guidance counselor

☐ Sign up for weekend tutoring

☐ Keep building forward

She looked at that last line. Thought about the ant from Proverbs, no drama, no announcements, just steady work every single day.

She clicked off the lamp.

Small steps. Real ones.

That was enough for tonight.

Chapter Seven

FRICTION

The red brick walls of her school looked different than she remembered.

Sakari stood on the sidewalk out front, fingers tight around her backpack strap, heart going faster than she wanted it to. She hadn't been back since the fire.

She walked in.

The hallway swallowed her up. Heads turned. Whispers broke out in small clusters behind her, the kind people think they're hiding but aren't. A few kids stared straight at her before looking away. She kept her eyes forward and her feet moving.

By third period, the day had the texture of walking through something thick. Every room felt louder than usual. Every glance landed a little harder. Even Angie was polite in a careful, distant way, friendly enough, but with a wall behind it.

Sakari kept going anyway.

The gym whistle cut through the noise.

"Flag football!" the teacher called out. "Let's move!"

Sakari drifted toward the sideline. She hadn't brought the right shoes. She wasn't sure she was in the right headspace either.

"Johnson!" Coach's voice found her. "You in or out?"

Her palms were already damp. She thought about stepping back.

"In."

She jogged onto the field. The turf was soft and springy under her feet. The air smelled like rubber and sweat. Someone in the huddle handed her a red flag belt, stiff and barely used.

The game started.

She ran. Her lungs burned fast, she hadn't pushed herself like this in weeks. Her breath came in short bursts. Her legs found a rhythm anyway. She stayed with it.

She pulled two flags. On one play, she broke into open space, caught a short pass, and crossed the cone they were using as the end zone.

Someone on the sideline clapped.

A teammate jogged past her, grinning. "Didn't know you had wheels like that."

Sakari bent forward, hands on her knees, catching her breath. "Me neither."

Her dad picked her up after school in a loaner car from the relief fund. She climbed in and dropped her bag at her feet.

"How was it?" he asked, pulling out of the lot.

"Good." She thought about it. "Weird. But good."

He nodded, eyes on the road. "Going back took guts."

They rode without talking for a few minutes. The comfortable kind of quiet, no tension in it, just two people in a car watching the neighborhood go by.

Then he said, "One good day doesn't erase everything. But it's real."

Sakari nodded. "I know."

The words didn't sting this time. They just landed steady, like something she could stand on.

That night she sat on the hotel bed with the project slides open on her laptop and her checklist on the nightstand beside her. Angie had sent another round of edits. She needed to get through them.

Her mind kept drifting.

The whispers in the hallway. The careful way Angie smiled. The friend who still hadn't texted back.

She pulled herself back, opened the slides, and worked through them one by one. When she finished, she picked up the pen.

✔ Gym class

✔ Project edits

She looked at the next item.

☐ Talk to Mom.

She clicked the pen open and closed a few times. Then set it down and got up.

Her mom was in the kitchenette, working through a pile of donated clothes from the relief center. Sweaters and jeans in all different sizes, folded into soft stacks.

"Can I help?" Sakari asked from the doorway.

Her mom looked up. A small surprise crossed her face. "Sure."

They folded without talking. Matching sleeves, smoothing fronts, stacking by size. The rhythm of it felt easy.

Then Sakari said, "I know I still have a lot to make up for."

Her mom kept folding. Didn't answer right away.

"I know you're trying," she finally said.

"I just don't want the fire to be the only thing people remember about me." Sakari set a folded sweater on the pile. "I don't want it to be the whole story."

Her mom turned and looked at her directly. "Then make sure it isn't."

Four words. Sakari held onto them.

Back in the room, she opened her notebook to a fresh page and wrote one new line at the bottom of her checklist.

☐ Stay steady, even when it's hard.

Below that, smaller:

Growth doesn't always look like winning. But it still counts.

She read it back once. Closed the notebook. Turned off the lamp.

Tomorrow the friction would still be there, the whispers, the careful smiles, the long road back.

She planned to walk it anyway.

Chapter Eight
FORWARD MOTION

Saturday morning came in quietly.

No alarm. No scramble. Sakari was already up. She sat cross-legged at the hotel table, laptop open, checklist flat beside it. The TV stayed off. Her phone sat face-down on silent. Outside, the parking lot was still and gray.

Angie had sent the final project slides over last night. Sakari opened them now and read through every slide slowly, checking citations, fixing a font size on slide four, making sure the transitions made sense. She went through the whole deck twice.

Then she opened her email.

To: Mr. Hatala Final slides attached. Thank you for your patience.

She hovered over the send button.

A familiar voice stirred somewhere in the back of her head, the old one, the comfortable one. *You could look it over one more time. Wait until this afternoon. Make sure it's perfect.*

She recognized the voice for what it was.

She tapped send.

The email disappeared into the outbox. Done. Finished. No last-minute panic, no extension needed, no excuses waiting in the wings.

Just done.

She sat back and looked at the ceiling for a moment.

It felt better than she expected.

Her mom appeared in the doorway, still in her robe, coffee in hand. She looked at Sakari, then at the laptop, then back at Sakari.

"You're up early."

"Wanted to get the project in," Sakari said. "We present Monday."

Her mom stood there a beat longer than the question required. "We're proud of you. Your dad and me both."

Sakari smiled. "Thanks."

Her mom crossed the room and smoothed a wrinkle on the shoulder of Sakari's hoodie, a small, quiet gesture, then walked back out. The door clicked shut gently behind her.

Sakari looked at the sent email one more time.

Then she closed the laptop.

The rec center smelled like cardboard and dryer sheets and the faint plastic of new packaging. Fluorescent lights buzzed a steady hum overhead. Folding tables lined the walls, loaded with bins. Volunteers moved between them, calling across the room.

"Medium coats go in that bin!" "We need more gloves up front!"

A volunteer had asked Sakari to come back if she wanted more hours. She'd said yes on the spot.

Her assignment today was donations, sorting shoes, jackets, toiletries into the right piles. She worked through the bins steadily, checking sizes, grouping by type. Her hands stayed busy. Her mind stayed quiet.

Then a man and his son came through the door.

The boy was maybe seven. His jacket swallowed him whole, sleeves past his hands, collar up around his ears. His dad flipped through the outerwear bin with the careful, uncertain look of someone who didn't want to take more than his share.

"Is it okay to take two?" the dad asked, not looking up.

"Absolutely," Sakari said. "Take what you need."

She moved to the rack and flipped through the hangers until she found a navy puffer in the right size. "Try this one."

The boy shrugged it on and zipped it all the way up. His whole face changed. He stuck his arms straight out and spun in a slow circle, like he was testing whether it gave him powers.

His dad caught Sakari's eye and nodded. "Thank you."

She nodded back.

She stood there for a second after they moved on, watching the kid spin again near the door. Something in her chest felt settled and clear. She wasn't running from anything right now. She wasn't waiting for someone to notice her or tell her what to do.

She was just there, helping, and that was the whole point.

That night the four walls of the hotel room held something different: the smell of pizza and the sound of her whole family talking.

Cheap paper plates. Store-brand soda in plastic cups. Nobody complained. Her dad had one leg hanging off the edge of the bed. Her mom kept stealing his crust. Sakari ate two slices fast and then slowed down on the third.

Her dad looked at her between bites. "Monday's the big presentation?"

"Yep." She wiped her hands on a napkin. "I'm ready."

"You've come a long way in two weeks," he said.

Sakari shrugged. "Still got a ways to go."

He pointed at her with his slice. "Yeah. But you're moving."

She thought about that for the rest of the meal.

After dinner, she opened her notebook to a clean page.

Sunday

☐ Review slides one last time

☐ Prep outfit for presentation

☐ Call Nana back

☐ Help Dad with job search board

☐ Return library books

She looked at the list. Then added one more line at the bottom.

☐ Keep your eyes forward.

She meant it. No more circling back to the fire, no more sitting inside the guilt and letting it grow. That wasn't the same as forgetting, she'd never forget. But the fire was behind her.

Everything on this list was ahead.

She capped the pen, closed the notebook, and got ready for bed.

Monday was coming.

She was ready to meet it.

CHAPTER NINE

MOMENTUM AND MIRRORS

M onday came whether she was ready or not.
She didn't hit snooze.

Sakari sat up, stretched, and got dressed with intention, clean jeans, her black sweater, and the necklace Nana had mailed after the fire. Simple. Put together. She looked in the mirror and let herself look.

Her checklist sat folded in her backpack. She didn't open it. She already knew what the day held.

The school hallways moved the way they always did on Monday mornings, loud and scattered, everyone in their own orbit. Most people had no idea what it had taken her to walk back through these doors last week.

Sakari walked tall anyway.

She spotted Angie near the classroom door, flash drive already in hand.

"You have the intro?" Angie asked.

"And the closing."

They touched fists. Then walked in together.

The presentation moved better than Sakari had rehearsed it in her head.

She stood up, made eye contact with the room, and spoke clearly. Her notes stayed in order. Her voice stayed steady. When she got to the closing section, she felt the class actually listening, a few heads nodding, the room holding still in that way it does when something lands right.

Mr. Hatala smiled when they finished.

Angie leaned over on the way back to their seats and whispered, "Look at you. Being all responsible."

Sakari rolled her eyes. "Don't get used to it."

But she meant the opposite, and she was pretty sure Angie knew it.

At lunch she took her food outside to the old oak tree near the back of campus.

She used to come here to hide, to disappear when the noise inside got too heavy. She sat down in the same spot, back against the bark, legs stretched out in the grass.

It didn't feel like hiding today. It just felt like a good place to sit.

She pulled out her phone and scrolled back through Nana's texts from the weekend.

Proud of you.

Call soon.

You're made of good stuff, baby girl.

She read them twice. The phone screen caught the light and threw a faint reflection back at her, just her face, small and clear.

Not perfect. Getting there.

She put the phone in her pocket and finished her lunch in the quiet.

Her dad's loaner car was at the curb when she came out after school. He had his sleeves rolled up, a clipboard balanced on the dashboard.

"How'd it go?" he asked as she got in.

"We nailed it."

"That's what I like to hear."

He pulled out of the lot. A light drizzle started up, the kind that barely counts as rain, just enough to blur the windshield. He turned the wipers on low.

They pulled into the hotel lot and climbed out. Her mom was already standing at the entrance, holding something.

A letter. Taped to the door.

Sakari peeled it off and handed it over.

Her mom opened it slowly. Read it once. Then her whole face changed, something tight and tired letting go all at once.

"It's from the church," she said. "They're covering hotel costs for two more weeks while we look for something permanent."

Sakari stared at her. "Why?"

Her mom looked up. "Pastor's wife said someone was impressed with your work at the relief center."

The warmth spread through her chest before she could think about it. She stood there in the drizzle and let it settle.

Not a complete answer. Not a house back or a history undone. A bridge. Two weeks of solid ground to keep building from.

Sometimes that's exactly enough.

That night she lay on top of the hotel covers, staring at the ceiling, the day still buzzing in her chest.

She opened her notebook.

✔ Presentation

✔ Call Nana

✔ Help Dad

✔ Breathe

She sat with the list for a moment. Then wrote one new line underneath.

☐ Don't run from your reflection, grow into it.

She read it back. Closed the notebook.

Whispered, "Thank you," to the quiet room, not to anyone specific, just out into the air, because the feeling needed somewhere to go.

She turned off the lamp.

The drizzle tapped soft against the window.

Tomorrow was already on its way, and for the first time in a long time, she was facing the same direction.

CHAPTER TEN
THE HOME STRETCH

F riday afternoon light came through the classroom windows in long flat angles, warm and
unhurried. The week had moved in a blur, the presentation, volunteer shifts, slow careful conversations
with classmates, small pieces of trust rebuilt one day
at a time.

Sakari tapped her pencil against the edge of her desk
and waited.

Mr. Hatala moved through the rows handing back
the graded projects. When he reached her, he set the
paper down and smiled. "Solid work. Keep showing
up like this and your grades will follow."

She turned it over.

She looked at it for a long moment. Not a perfect
score. Every point on it was earned, though, earned

the real way, without shortcuts or last-minute panic or someone else carrying her half. She folded it and tucked it into her notebook.

That number meant something.

Her family was waiting in the hotel lobby after school. Her dad had a folded lease in one hand. Her mom held a set of keys, used, a little worn, two keys on a plain ring.

"It's not big," her mom said. "But it's ours."

They loaded into a borrowed van. Her dad had the address written on the back of a receipt: 212 Spring Oak Lane.

The rental was modest. Two bedrooms. Mismatched carpet, tan in the hallway, something close to green in the back room. The walls had scuff marks at chair height and a few small patches near the baseboards. The refrigerator buzzed steadily in the kitchen. A box fan hummed in the corner of the main room. A thrift-store lamp stood near the window and flickered once when her mom clicked it on, then held steady.

A card table sat where a dining set would eventually go.

The whole place smelled faintly of fresh paint.

Sakari walked through each room slowly. She looked at the scuff marks and the mismatched floors and the crack along the ceiling of the back bedroom.

She put her backpack down on her new bed.

Not a hotel cot. Not a couch cushion. A bed, hers, in a room with a door and a window and walls that belonged to her family.

She flopped back onto it and stared straight up at the ceiling crack.

She was smiling before she realized it.

The sheets were stiff from the package. The room had a small echo to it. The lamp in the corner wasn't quite bright enough.

None of that mattered.

That night she sat at the desk, chipped along one corner, solid everywhere else, and opened her notebook. She flipped past the checklists and the hotel notepad pages, past the ant verse she'd copied down and the list she'd made the night of the fire.

She found a blank page.

She wrote across the top:

New Chapter.

Then below it:

✔ Present the project

✔ Rebuild trust

✔ Volunteer hours

✔ Stay consistent

She looked at the list. Then at the bottom of the page, she wrote one more line, the same one she'd been writing and rewriting for three weeks, but it meant something different now.

☐ Keep building forward.

She set her pen down and looked around the room.

A box of books she would actually organize. A dresser that would hold clothes she would actually keep folded. A ceiling crack that caught the lamplight in a way that looked almost like a line on a map.

Three weeks ago she would have seen everything wrong with this room. She would have seen the scuff marks and the mismatched carpet and the flickering lamp and called it not enough.

Now she saw a place to start.

She thought about the ant, no announcement, no waiting for perfect conditions, just steady movement every single day. Building something real one small piece at a time.

She closed her notebook.

The refrigerator buzzed in the kitchen. The box fan turned slowly in the corner. Somewhere outside, a car passed and its headlights swept across the ceiling.

Sakari sat in the quiet of her new room and felt, for the first time in a long time, exactly where she was supposed to be.

Small steps. Real ones.

She was ready.